Pit's
SALVATION

SAINT'S OUTLAWS MC

Pit's
SALVATION

NAT LOGAN

President: Gavin "Pit" Lawson

Vice President: Justice

Sgt at Arms: Tack

Enforcer: Stinger

Road Captain: Retread

Chaplain: Crux

Treasurer: Cash

Secretary: Sledge

Members: Cuffs, Gator, Cue, Deputy Dawg

Ol' Ladies: Ariel Lawson

Badass, Fierce Women widowed: Charlotte Lawson (Charlie or Chuck), Ruth Lawson (Ruthless)

President: Warrick "War" Shields
Vice President: Benton "Bear" Carter
Sgt at Arms: Moss "Cannon" Adler
Enforcer: Jason "Cruise" Parks
Road Captain: Speedy
Tech: Derek "Scoop" Layton
Medic: Flick
Chaplain: Noah "Locks" Franks
Treasurer: Matthew "Roam" Shields
Secretary: Slice
Members: Dex
Originals: Rascal (father to Bear), Baron (father to War, Roam, Gage, Ariel)
Nomad: Compass, Booker, Twist
Ol' Ladies: Regina Shields, Remington Shields, Winchester Carter, Sarah Layton, Meg Carter, Sprite Jones, Jesse Adler, Willa Parks
Badass, Fierce Women unclaimed: Beth Franks, Stella Layton, Rose Layton, Tasha Layton, Kennedy, Clara, Della

President: Bootstrap
Vice President: Gage "Brew" Shields
Sgt at Arms: Open
Enforcer: Salty
Road Captain: Dodge
Tech: Cowboy
Medic: Open
Chaplain: Open
Treasurer: Donner
Secretary: Blue

DEDICATION

This book is dedicated to my amazing ARC team. I am grateful for your support.

TABLE OF CONTENT

CHAPTER ONE

Gavin "Pit" Lawson woke up as the warm, curvy body slid in beside his. How she circumvented his security system and got in each time was a mystery to him. They'd been doing this dance for over three months, and although he enjoyed every second of their time together, he craved more. He wanted dinners out with her. He wanted her on the back of his motorcycle on club runs. At his age, he'd had all the easy, no-strings sex he wanted, and he was tired of it. With her, it was so much more. If he was going to have a family and actually get to be able to see them grow up, he needed to get a move on. When he was younger, he would have scoffed at finding love at fifty-three, but he'd been bowled over when she'd rolled into his life.

As President of the Saint's Outlaws MC, Kansas City, KS Chapter, he wasn't used to not getting his way, but the woman he'd fallen for was one of the most stubborn, badass women he'd ever met—which said a lot considering who his mother was.

When his dad's MC chapter had been almost wiped out back in nineteen eighty-eight, his mom, along with a couple of the originals, held the club together and came up with a plan to keep them safe until Pit was old enough and experienced enough to take over. Pit and his friends had all joined the Army just like they'd planned after high school and served for eight years. His mom had taken his dad's place in the club, running it until Pit came back. It had been unconventional, but she'd done it. Then, before Pit came back, she'd approached an old Army friend of his dad's to see if they'd be willing to patch over their club with Pit taking over as president. Man, the balls of his mother.

Now, years later, their club was still a one-percenter club, but it was only because Pit considered the law more of a hindrance to justice sometimes. They didn't touch any human trafficking, drugs, or murder. In fact, they actively worked against it. Now, their gun store had a legitimate side and a not-so-legitimate side. Pit didn't agree with the gun laws and had no problem helping someone defend themselves.

A slim, feminine hand slid into his chest hair and then drifted down his chest, bringing his thoughts back to the beauty in his bed. Of course, his cock was on board with whatever she wanted. He couldn't resist her, and neither could his cock. If Pit had more willpower, he'd force her hand. But he was worried if he did, she'd never show up again, and he couldn't handle that.

He inhaled her scent and wondered how long she was in town for. Her job had her going all over, and he hungered to have her by his side. If he could tattoo *MINE* all over her, he would. She was his, but she just didn't know it yet. He just had to figure out how to make it happen.

"Does your dad know you're here?" Pit asked.

Ariel Shields flipped the bedside light on, then grasped his hands, holding them above his head as she settled herself astride his abdomen.

"Are you freaking kidding me?" Ariel said, rolling her eyes. "My dad knows I'm freaking forty years old and doesn't worry about whose bed I'm in. Are you trying to rile me up tonight, old man?"

Ouch. She knew how sensitive he was about being thirteen years older than her, and she'd gone for the jugular with her words. He bucked underneath her, knocking her off balance enough to slide her down to rub against his aching cock. He leaned up, nipping at her breast through the thin T-shirt she'd worn to bed.

"I'm trying to figure out how to get my woman to let me claim her and tell the world. The nighttime visits are hot as hell, but I want more. You sneaking out the back before anyone sees you is frustrating."

Although Pit didn't live in the clubhouse, his house was on the property, which made it even more annoying that Ariel was able to get in and out without any of their security going off.

"What if I don't want to be claimed but want to claim you?"

Pit snickered, then laughed. Ariel let go of his hands, and he pulled them down and set them on her waist. He'd been humoring her by letting her feel like she was controlling him.

"Don't laugh at me, oh ancient one."

Her name for him had him chuckling louder, which had her gorgeous face turning red. She'd grown up with three overprotective older brothers and had a little bit of an attitude if someone dismissed her abilities. Heck, she was lethal, and he'd never dismiss her prowess.

"I'm not laughing at you." He slid his hand up her waist, then pulled her toward him. "I was chuckling because you've already claimed me, and I've claimed you. Do you honestly believe I'd allow anyone to touch the woman who has burrowed her way into every last little part of my heart? You wouldn't expect anything less than what your parents have, which is what I want too. It all hinges on you finally wanting more than these late-night booty calls."

His lips ghosted over hers and slid down her neck. She shivered in his arms, and he rolled them over quickly before she could stop him. He pressed down until he was allowing almost all his weight on her.

"Do you want more, Sugar? Are you ready to give me all I want?" he whispered, licking and nibbling down her body. Her quiet moan told him she was enjoying it, but he needed her to want more. He kissed and caressed, sliding her panties down her thighs as he traced each inch of the satiny skin he unveiled.

He tossed her panties toward the chair in his room and looked at her. Her dark brown hair was splayed across his pillow. Her toffee-colored eyes stared at him with hunger. She was still a little self-conscious of her body even though he told her how much he loved her curves. She'd slipped on one of his T-shirts before coming to bed. She worked out to keep in shape for her job, but she still had a bubble butt and what she called her Buddha-belly, which, no matter what she did, would never be hard. He loved every soft inch of her and told her this endlessly. He laid kisses on her ankle, moving up her leg, enjoying tasting and touching every satiny inch of her. A loud banging and the doorbell ringing had him closing his eyes for a second.

"Please let me be imagining that sound," he said.

Ariel giggled. "If you are, I am too. It sounds like Sledge is trying to get your attention."

Pit figured it was him too because he always knocked like he was knocking down a door to fight a fire, which made sense because Sledge was a fireman. Pit slid on his jeans and grabbed his gun from the nightstand. Ariel was getting dressed. He wondered if he'd return to find her ghosted from the area. He'd hoped he could convince her tonight to let people know about them and take the next step. He slid to the side of his door but leaned to look through the peephole. He wasn't sure what was going on, but some of his brothers were on his front porch at one in the morning, along with some of the Bluff Creek Brotherhood MC.

Neither boded well for him getting back in bed with Ariel anytime soon tonight.

He opened the door and hoped this didn't turn into the clusterfuck he was imagining it could.

"Sorry, Pit. I called and texted, but you didn't answer. Baron, Roam, and War are concerned about Ariel."

Pit waved his arm toward his family room to have them join him. He wasn't sure how much more this could get screwed up. Ariel was the woman he'd imagined in his life since the moment he'd seen her in a bar. But she ghosted in and out on her assignments, never staying more than a night or two. He was positive he meant more to her than just a string of one-night stands, but she wasn't one of those women who shared stuff. She kept everything locked down.

He sat down and waited for the men to start.

"Why are you here?" Pit asked when no one said anything after a few minutes, looking at Ariel's dad and two of her brothers. Brew was the Vice President in their Texas Chapter and hadn't made the trip. Ariel's dad, Baron, was one of the originals who started Bluff Creek Brotherhood MC. He'd been the President until he'd handed it over to his son, War. Roam was War's twin and served as the Treasurer for their club. He also ran the club's tattoo shop and had done some of the tattoos Pit sported. Baron, War, and Roam were closer because they were at the original chapter in Bluff Creek, Kansas.

"Well, I was concerned about Ariel last time she swept through town. She was secretive, and so I had Scoop give me some trackers to install on her vehicle and items she used a lot," War explained.

Awww man, this is not how Pit wanted his friends to find out that he was having sex with their sister and daughter. He'd been hoping that Ariel would agree for them to go public. He was going to make a drive to Bluff Creek, explain how he felt about her, and ask for Baron's blessing. It might seem old-fashioned, but since he'd basically been having sex with the princess of Bluff Creek behind their backs, it seemed like the least he could do.

Banging on his door had him wondering who else would be screwing up his life tonight.

Crux, another one of his brothers, their Chapter's Chaplain and the manager of their gun range, opened the door. It might seem like those jobs didn't all mix, but Crux made them work.

"Hey, Pit. Looks like you have some more visitors."

The grin Crux was trying to hide had Pit wanting to kick his Chaplain, but that was frowned upon.

Remington, War's wife and also the head of Franks and Daughters Bail Bonds, walked in along with a couple of her sisters. Sarah was the bail bonds tech person, and Beth was their surveillance expert. With what he'd learned from Ariel, besides working with them, she considered them all good friends.

"Remi, what are you doing here? This is club business."

Remi rolled her eyes and walked over to her husband, then thumped him on his ear before he knew what she was doing.

"What the hell, Remi?"

"Oh, so it's club business. Explain to me how club business includes putting trackers on your sister's stuff when she's a grown woman." Remi's glare could have melted metal, and Pit was wholeheartedly glad he wasn't on the receiving end of it.

"Remi, War was just doing what I asked. I was worried about Ariel," Baron said.

Remi rolled her eyes and stared at Baron.

"I don't believe I've ever been as disappointed in you three as I am today. Did any of you three think to directly ask Ariel what she was doing? Or where she was going? Or did you just decide she was the club princess who couldn't take care of herself and the big, strong men would keep track of her?"

Pit shuddered at the sarcasm dripping from Remi's words. He'd worked with Remi multiple times when their interests of saving women intersected. She was a badass just like his Sugar was. Ariel rolled her eyes sometimes when he called her that, but he was positive she loved it. He'd told her why he was calling her that pet name the first time they got together. She was sweet as sugar but could be hard as steel when needed.

"Now, Remi..." War started.

"Don't 'now Remi' me, you neanderthal."

"Remi, you know that older brothers need to watch out for their sisters," Roam stated, trying to back up his twin.

Remi shook her head again. Then hit a button on her phone, sending a text, he assumed. His door opened, a-gain, only this time, Pit was ready to hide. Pit had known that if Baron was mad at him for sleeping with Ariel, then they could settle it in the ring. Now, with Baron's wife, Regina, here, he wasn't sure what the outcome of tonight would be.

"What do you three think you're doing?" Regina asked, with her arms crossed, tapping her foot as she waited for their answer.

"Regina, we've been worried about Ariel. She's barely come home since the boys returned. And she doesn't check in that often," Baron said.

"With you," Regina said.

"What?" Baron asked.

"With you. She doesn't check in with you because every time she calls, you always put a guilt trip on her that she doesn't call enough or come home enough. She and I text and chat every week."

Pit hid his smile behind his hand because he really didn't want to get beat up tonight. But seeing Regina's strength, he was getting a glimpse of how Ariel would handle their sons in years to come, if they were blessed with them. He could see Regina had obviously passed down the steel spine to her daughter.

Baron stared at Regina, then asked, "Why didn't you share what she said?"

"You never asked me about Ariel. I'm guessing you and your two thick-headed sons were too busy planning how the big, strong men would keep Ariel safe. I love the three of you and your protectiveness," War started to smile then paused when Regina continued, "but she's not a baby. Sure, she's your younger sister, but she is a strong, fierce forty-year-old woman who is friggin' amazing at her job."

"But she doesn't say exactly what she does," War sputtered.

"She told you she works at the bail bonds in investigations. What more do you want her to tell you?" Remi asked.

"But what exactly does that mean?" Baron asked.

"She investigates things we need investigated. What more do you need explained?" Remi replied.

Pit couldn't see where this was going, but he was a tad concerned that the club's relationship with Bluff Creek Brotherhood MC might be damaged. Ariel was going to be his wife and Ol' Lady, but he'd hoped to be able to control how War, Baron, and Roam found out. Now, it was anyone's guess how this would turn out.

"So why come here?" Pit questioned.

He felt a little stupid focusing their interest back on him, but he wasn't sure how he fit in.

"Well, we don't check that often. Most times when we check, we see the tracker in Topeka, where one of the bail bonds offices is, or in Texas a couple of times, but then today, we saw she was in Kansas City. Then four trackers started all going different ways. One went toward Colorado. One went toward Chicago. The other two went south on Interstate thirty-five and then split, one east on Highway Forty and one west. We decided to see if we could stay here and then start trying to figure out what happened," Baron said.

"How about we all go get some sleep and then we can talk about it tomorrow? I can guarantee that Ariel is fine," Beth Franks, the youngest sister of the bail bonds, stated.

"How can you guarantee she's fine when the trackers are all going different directions?" War asked.

"Well, they're all going different directions because Ariel was angry when I called to tell her about them," Beth stated, grinning at War.

"How did you find out about them?" War asked.

"Sarah saw them on Scoop's laptop when her husband left the program up and running when he went to the bathroom. She was a little irritated at the high-handedness of you guys," Beth stated.

This wasn't getting better, and Pit was worried this would be an epic explosion they couldn't come back from.

"How about Sledge and Crux get you all either rooms in the clubhouse or into our cabins to stay the night? I'm sure everyone is tired. Then we can sit down tomorrow and see if you all still need help."

Pit was really hoping they'd take him up on his offer. He hadn't heard any sounds from the bedroom and really hoped Ariel didn't walk out now.

"We'd love a cabin, Pit. Remi, Sarah, Beth, and I can stay together. I have no wish to sleep beside my husband tonight since he obviously didn't want to let me in on his plans," Regina stated.

He nodded at Crux. "Ladies, come with me. Do you have luggage we need to get?" Crux said as he led them out of the house.

Baron, War, and Roam stood up. "Sorry to barge in, Pit. When I saw all those trackers going different ways, all I could think about was a human trafficking ring trying to get rid of evidence. We'll stay in the clubhouse, and I'm sure I'll be trying to figure out how to get in my wife's good graces tomorrow," War said.

"Sledge will get you set up, and there's no reason to apologize. I can see how it would scare you. We can all get together tomorrow morning."

Pit waited until he saw the guys go in the back door of the clubhouse before he closed and locked his door, turning off the lights as he made his way back to his room. He walked into his bedroom. Ariel was sitting on the bed.

"Well, this seems a fine situation we're in," Pit said.

Ariel giggled, then fell over chuckling on the bed.

"Oh my gosh. Your face when they were talking. How they didn't see the fear in your eyes was beyond me. Now what do I get for not coming out there and blowing everything up tonight?" Ariel said, smiling.

CHAPTER TWO

Ariel had listened in while Regina and some of her friends put her dad and brothers in their place. Her dad and brothers only had themselves to blame for not knowing exactly what Ariel did.

Back when she had graduated college, she mentioned to her dad that she was interested in making a difference. Despite him saying over the years that she could do anything she wanted, he kept mentioning how she needed to have a safe job.

She'd walked into Franks and Daughters Bail Bonds and spoke to Remi about what she was interested in. She'd also talked with

Remi about how she had trouble staying on one task for an extended period of time. She worked best when she had different stimuli and things to figure out.

Remi had welcomed her with open arms and said they could tailor a job to fit her skillset and her personality. Remi didn't see the need to protect her or to limit her ability to work with the company. Ariel had trained and completed all the courses the bail bonds required, and then she'd spent time training directly with the Franks sisters.

Not only was she proficient in investigations, but Ariel had actually been the one to train Beth Franks in surveillance since Beth was younger.

Ariel watched Pit stalking toward her, pulling off his T-shirt and tossing it onto the chair in his room. He might be fifty-three, but he kept in shape. He had some gray hairs coming in on his chest and some in his beard, but it only made him hotter to her.

Ariel was a little irritated at her family for busting in because she'd planned on talking to Pit this weekend about where they were going from here. Now it wouldn't seem like her idea; it would sound like she was doing it in response to her dad and brothers. However, she'd already spoken to Remi about how she'd like her job to change. Ariel wanted to be based in Kansas City. For now, she'd still run investigations online and in person, but if Pit ended up wanting the same things she did, then she'd move to only online. When she had kids, she planned on being a mom who was around. And with Pit's age, she was positive he'd want to get started right away.

His hands on her ankles, tugging her toward the end of the bed knocked all the thoughts of the future out of her mind. Dang, this man did it for her. His deep blue eyes and grin had pulled her in.

The fact that her man was heavily endowed in the manhood area and knew how to use it was a fantastic bonus. When Pit had her close to the end of the bed, he let go of her ankles, grasped the neck of his T-shirt she was wearing, and ripped it down the middle. Holy cow, that was hot. The wetness between her legs and her nipples pebbling had her wishing he'd just jump to the part where he thrust inside her and made them one.

"Don't think you're going to smile at me and make me forget about tasting my pussy. For once, I'm taking my time."

Okay, he knew her too well. So sue her because she loved to have him inside her fast, hard, and letting her know how much he wanted her. He slid her ankles over his shoulders and dropped to the ground between her legs. His warm breath and the touch of his lips had her pushing closer. He made her lose her mind each time he touched her. She couldn't stay quiet. Each touch and swipe of his tongue had everything coalescing between her legs, building until she was screaming *Gavin, please.* He smiled against her, then kissed his way up her body, pausing near her belly button to suck the skin.

From the first, he'd been obsessed with marking her skin. She was positive it was his way of reminding her she was his when she went away. She didn't need the reminders, but she loved them. His lips and tongue devoured the peaks of her breasts until her nipples were hard pebbles.

"Love your lush body and these curves. I could sleep on your tits if you let me."

At least he'd called them tits. She'd stopped in the middle of a blowjob for him when he'd called them knockers. Knockers weren't sexy. Tits she could live with. Pit had grown up in a rough MC and lost his dad right as he graduated high school. Between that and his time in the Army, he'd had to harden his exterior, but she knew the softy underneath. The man who fixed stuff for his mama at her house and still kissed her on the cheek every time he saw her.

"Well, I might let you if I was still able to breathe. Now, Gavin, friggin' fuck me. I want you inside me."

He kissed her lips and rolled them over until she was on top. "Maybe we should pause a minute and talk about us going forward."

She stared at him. He was freaking serious. She grabbed his hand. "Gavin, do you feel how wet I am? I ache for you, and you want to discuss tomorrow?"

His fingers slid around her clit and a couple of them plunged inside her, rubbing the spot that almost had her eyes crossing.

"No, I want to discuss you officially being my Ol' Lady and wife. Then I want to slide inside you, knowing you're mine permanently."

She tried to concentrate but his fingers inside her were making it hard.

"Can we talk about this later? After?" she moaned.

His fingers stopped. He didn't pull them out, just left them inside her, not moving.

His stern face let her know she wasn't getting him inside her until she answered.

"Tomorrow, I'll set up a time to meet my dad and brothers off property to show them I'm okay. You set up a family barbecue for tomorrow evening. I'll arrive. You can ask me to marry you and wear your cut. I'll accept and we'll get married on Sunday here."

Pit stared at her. She'd just given him everything he wanted, but she wanted it too.

"How are we going to get a marriage license by then?"

"Oh, get that look off your face. I know you have connections. I'll send out a text to the rest of Bluff Creek tomorrow, but especially Brew, so he has time to get here," Ariel said.

Pit slid his fingers out of her and notched his cock at her entrance.

"I accept," he said and thrust up into her.

Finally. Gavin could be so stubborn, but he always took care of her. She moved and watched his face as her breasts bounced as she rode him. He groaned her name and reached up to play with her nipples. He was close and knew exactly how to make sure the woman he loved came with him. The heat pooled, and she screamed *I love you* as she shook on top of him. Gavin followed immediately after. She leaned down against him. He held her, then turned his mouth to her ear.

"Sugar, we didn't use a condom this time. I'm sorry I didn't think about it."

She turned her head, brushing a kiss against his lips. "I figured you would want a family right away, so you definitely should marry me on Sunday!"

CHAPTER THREE

Ariel had snuck out of Pit's house before dawn. He'd gotten up with her, kissed her goodbye, and watched her until she disappeared into the compound. As she'd left, he'd growled that she needed to show him the vulnerability in their system so he could fix it.

She wondered how he'd feel when he realized it was a backdoor to their security system that they'd bought from her company. When Ariel had started working for the bail bonds, she and Remi had spent a large amount of time together. When Ariel had mentioned some of the weaknesses in the security at the bail bonds compound, Remi had challenged her to write or make a better one. Ariel had accepted the challenge. When she'd come back with the ideas and prototypes later, Remi had fronted her the money to incorporate and have her own company. Ariel had paid Remi back over the last ten years until Ariel now owned all of her company.

Even if Ariel never worked again, she could survive on her salary from her company. Ariel texted her mom, dad, and brothers to meet her at seven a.m. at IHOP at Legends Outlets Mall. When Ariel had started seeing Pit three months ago, she'd moved her base of operations to the Homewood Suites by the Kansas City Speedway. There was a small kitchen in the room and plenty of places to eat out. Most of the time, she moved around because she enjoyed it. Between the safe houses the non-profit connected to the bail bonds had and vacation rentals, she chose whatever would work for her job. She had a company SUV and then also had bought a new-to-her Harley Davidson sport bike to get around town. Her Iron 883 was perfect for her size.

She parked her bike and then headed into the hotel. She was on the fourth floor because she would rather be higher up and not have young kids jumping on her ceiling. She opened her door and tossed her keys on the table, kicking the extra plate out to keep the maids out of her room. Her place was on a special cleaning schedule but a couple times she'd been surprised when someone new started.

She dropped her clothing and flicked on the shower. Catching sight of Gavin's love bite on her brought a smile to her face.

Her thighs were a little sore from when she'd woken him with a blowjob during the night. He'd given her a couple minutes of control, then flipped her onto her back, slid her legs up until her feet were by his face, and proceeded to pound her until she screamed his name again. Her thighs weren't quite used to being that close to her own face, but when he'd leaned down to kiss her, she'd just lived with the burn of unused muscles.

She shampooed her hair and washed her body, thinking through how best to deal with her dad and brothers. She wanted to set it up so they didn't hold anything against Gavin. She finished showering and wrapped her hair in a towel, then dried off. She'd get ready and then make sure she was at the restaurant first. Establishing territory was the first step to controlling the narrative.

Ariel read a couple more pages of her book, and then her timer went off. She glanced at her watch: six-fifty-five a.m. She looked to the parking lot and saw her family minus Brew, who was still in Texas, walking in.

War glanced around the room and started to head toward a back booth on the other side of the restaurant. Her mom saw her and motioned for War to where she was sitting. Oh, Mr. MC President was not going to like that she picked the booth where she could see the parking lot and the entrance. Only one of them would be able to see even close to her line of sight.

"Morning. Hey, why don't you scoot over so we can all fit?" War said.

She wasn't falling for his maneuvering of her. As she started to give him a piece of her mind, Remi, Sarah, and Beth walked in the door and headed for their table.

"Nope, I'm good where I'm at. I'm sure everyone can find a seat," Ariel relayed and waited to see what War would do.

He grunted and took the next best seat. Once everyone was seated, Ariel motioned the waiter over.

"I'd like more coffee all around, and I'll take French toast and bacon."

Everyone else ordered. Immediately after the waiter left, War turned toward her.

"Spill it."

Ariel just stared at her older brother. She loved all her brothers, but she wasn't in high school anymore. They were all adults, and they needed to understand she wasn't going to be treated as a child. War's face blushed when she didn't immediately answer.

"Hey, it's good to see you. I think what War meant to say is how have you been doing, and we're sorry we put trackers on your vehicle."

She giggled. Leave it to Roam to try to be the peacemaker. She'd cut War some slack, but he'd need to see her as an adult.

"I've been doing great. I would have been happy to answer any questions about my job. I guess I don't remember anyone but Mom asking. But since you're asking now, I've met someone, and I can't wait for you to meet him."

Her dad sat forward in his seat. "We'd love to meet who you're dating. When?"

Her dad's and War's phones beeped with a text message. Pit was right on time.

"When do you want? It looks like Pit is having a barbecue for the whole MC, us, and anyone we want to invite tonight. I can tell Pit no if you were planning on tonight."

Ariel acted like she was pondering it. "You know, let's meet at the barbecue."

"Perfect." War's satisfaction in his tone was almost more than she could stomach. Sometimes older brothers were seriously annoying. She couldn't wait to see his face when he realized who her man was.

Ariel enjoyed the meal after the issue of her significant other was out of the way. Her brothers and dad asked more in-depth questions about what she did for the bail bonds. She loved talking about her job, especially when the guys were listening. Then she decided why not get it all out in the open and told them about her company. When she was at the part about Remi going in with her, War turned his head toward her like she'd betrayed him. Ariel had actually giggled when Remi had reminded him they hadn't been together yet.

The only thing that would have made her day better was if Brew could have been there for breakfast. After they finished, she asked the women if they'd like to go shopping with her later. If she was getting married tomorrow, she wanted at least a cute dress. They made plans to get together later, and then she headed out to her car.

She paused and then decided she'd swear Brew to secrecy.

> **Ariel: Do you promise to keep a secret?**

She waited for Brew to reply. Bluff Creek was three hours from the Saint's Outlaws MC. Brew was at their Cider Creek Chapter, and it was another five hours farther away than Bluff Creek. If she wanted him here tomorrow for the wedding, she'd need to tell him today.

Brew: Haven't I always unless it endangered you?

Ariel: Okay, I need you at the Saint's Outlaws MC clubhouse in Kansas City tomorrow, no later than one-thirty. Also, how about you bring at least two coolers full of Bluff Creek Brews? The ceremony will be casual, so just nice clean jeans.

Brew: Ceremony?

Ariel: I've been dating Pit and have fallen in love with him. We're getting married tomorrow.

Brew: Pit, the President of SOMC?

Ariel: Is there another Pit?

Brew: Don't be a smartass. Who knows?

Ariel: Only Pit and I know we're getting married tomorrow until Mom, Dad, War, and Roam find out tonight at the party. Long story, they showed up because the tagging they put on my vehicle went wonky.

Brew: How mad were you?

Ariel: I sent each of the four trackers in different directions.

Her phone rang and she picked up. "Hello."

"Hey, does he treat you right?" Brew's deep voice asked.

"Yeah, he does. He's everything I've always dreamed of. Can you make it?"

"Nothing could stop me. What time's the party and the big reveal? If I hurry, I can be there for that."

Brew had been the brother she'd grown up with. Roam and War had already been serving when she was in high school, but she and Brew had been there for each other. She was so glad he could make it because she couldn't imagine getting married without him there.

"Seven p.m. Thanks for coming."

"You know I wouldn't miss it. Love you."

Ariel stared at the phone and then pulled out of the parking lot. She had a little bit to get done before tonight.

CHAPTER FOUR

Pit scrutinized the area. If he was going to finally get to have Ariel with his men, he wanted it perfect. Of course, if Baron, War, and Roam all tried to kill him, he hoped the bloodbath wasn't too bad. He'd already supervised the meat in the smoker. He made sure Cue was following his directions exactly. Considering his road name came about from winning barbecue contests as Pitmaster, he definitely wasn't going to let one of his members screw up the barbecue for his engagement party. He'd considered ordering the food from his barbecue restaurant, Pit's KC Barbecue. Cue, short for barbecue, had some knowledge before he joined the MC, but Pit had taught him a lot, and Cue now helped Pit manage the club's barbecue place.

His mom and his aunt had just arrived, and they were making a beeline for him. He was positive his mom and aunt would adore Ariel. She was tough like they were. Of course, his mom and aunt didn't have a choice. When most of the men were wiped out, they could have just run and made a life somewhere else. Instead, his mom, his aunt, and a couple of the guys who were left had set a plan to give their MC a chance to recover.

His mom had always been involved in the business, but suddenly she and his aunt had everything in their laps. His mom was seventy-five. She'd had him when she was twenty-two. She'd been the quintessential biker chick, and she still dressed that way. She didn't care what anyone thought of her. Although her given name was Charlotte, his MC family and her friends called her Chuck. The nickname had helped when she was dealing with people because she'd actually threatened people with, 'Don't make me call Chuck.'

Her arms wrapped around him, and she pulled him tight. After they lost so many people, she'd always greeted him or sent him on his way with a hug. She'd regretted that she'd been busy and hadn't given his dad the goodbye he deserved because she'd been distracted with a task. He leaned close to kiss her cheek.

"How's my boy?" she asked.

"I'm good. Everything's set."

He'd decided to let his mom and aunt in on what was happening. He might need them to help diffuse the situation. When he'd told his mom who he was going to make his Ol' Lady and wife, she grinned, then shook her head, teasing him that he never did anything easy.

He was most concerned because SOMC was a one-percenter club and Bluff Creek Brotherhood MC wasn't. Pit's club didn't traffic women, sell drugs, or anything like that. Heck, most of his members were in law enforcement or first responders, but Pit and his men didn't believe the law always helped the innocent. Sometimes, justice needed a little help.

His cousin and the Vice President of his club walked over. Justice picked up his mom, kissing her cheek and spinning her around.

"Justice, what have you done? You only try to distract me with that when you've done something you shouldn't," Ruth asked.

Very few people knew that his Aunt Ruth was the SOMC boogeyman, Ruthless, that the club had threatened people with for the years Pit and his brothers were gone. A couple months after the guys had left for the Army, a small group of men had attacked the compound, trying to burn down what was left. A small figure completely covered in black was seen right before all the men were gunned down. All her mom's statements to the police and fire department included this supposed vigilante who had protected the club.

From there, when something happened that hurt some other organization that had threatened SOMC, his mom and Ruth blamed it on the vigilante, whether Ruthless had done it or not. His mom had used it to their advantage to protect herself and her family.

"Mama, I haven't done anything," Justice whined.

"Hey, Justice. Somebody's looking for you," Tack teased.

Tack was Justice's younger brother and also a first responder with SWAT. The boys could get stuff done but during their off time, the pranks they played sometimes bordered on juvenile. Pit let it happen because with their jobs, letting off steam was a good thing.

"Who?" Justice asked.

"Your future wife," Tack teased, then pulled his mom over to kiss her cheek.

"Justice, is there something you need to tell me?" Ruth asked.

Justice backed away, shaking his head. "No, Mama. Just someone who doesn't understand the word 'no.' I'll take care of it."

Pit had no idea what Justice had done now, but at least for a little while, he'd relaxed before the main event.

"Bluff Creek's here, and it looks like it's both chapters. I see Brew along with his President, Bootstrap," his mom whispered.

He and his mom walked toward the Shields and the rest of the group to welcome them. *Please let this go okay.* He was deferring to his future wife instead of trying to control everything. She knew her family best. He hoped.

Ariel had decided that biker chick chic was how she was meeting all of Pit's family and friends. She knew Pit's group had women hanging around the clubhouse. She'd heard one of the guys refer to the women who stayed at the club as Sirens. Pit had explained that although he hadn't availed himself of them since they'd got together, he had previously. They treated the Sirens differently, though. The girls couldn't just come live there. They had to have a plan for a job or already hold an outside job. The club would help them with college or technical school if they wanted to attend. The Sirens were also required to help with cleaning and cooking. Pit had mentioned his mom and aunt had decided to change their jobs when the club was rebuilding.

She rode up to the clubhouse gates on her motorcycle. The prospect at the gate waited until she stopped. She flipped up her face shield so he could see her face.

"I'm here for the party."

"Name?" he asked.

"Ariel."

At her name, he straightened. She had to admit she'd only given her first name as a little test to see if Pit had impressed on the guys who she was. He'd passed with flying colors, which she'd known he would.

"Pit said you can pull around right there and park." The prospect indicated the place beside where she could see Pit's bike parked. He seemed to know her pretty well. The place beside his bike wasn't big enough for her SUV to park. She nodded at the prospect and rode toward the spot. She backed her bike in and then shut her down.

"I've got this," Ariel muttered to herself. Now she was freaking resorting to pep talks.

She'd gone over fifty different ways to tell her parents who her man was, but she still didn't know which way to go. They all had the possibility of creating a scene, so she'd wait until she walked in to see what felt right. She left her helmet on her seat. If anybody touched it, she'd teach them a lesson, but she wasn't worried. Pit kept everyone in line.

It was now or never. She shook her hair out and then threw her shoulders back. Time to claim her man. She strode around the edge of the clubhouse, moving through the different people hanging around. She recognized all the members because she'd familiarized herself with them. Pit was standing by her dad and brothers. Not only had Brew made it but it looked like most of the guys from Cider Creek had come too. Well, that settled it. She was going for the all-out drama. She smiled and walked toward them. Her dad and brothers smiled but were looking behind her. When she got closer, she could tell they were getting a little irritated that they couldn't see anyone. When she was a couple feet away, she smiled at Pit and ran, jumping up into his arms. He caught her, but she didn't give him time to say anything. She plastered her lips against his, then tilted her head and kissed him, sliding her tongue into his mouth. No one would misunderstand what she was screaming with her actions.

At the cheering and wolf whistles, she pulled away a little, leaning her forehead against his.

"Honey, I'm home," she said.

Pit grinned. "Yes, you are."

Keeping her in his arms, Pit turned toward her family.

"We've been together for three months, and she is everything to me. She'll be my wife, my Ol' Lady, my partner, and my salvation."

His words meant the world to her. He wasn't a man for fancy talk or talking about his emotions. It was hard for him, but for her, he'd bared his soul to her family and his.

War sputtered, "What? How? When? What the hell?"

Ariel laughed. "Do you really want to know how?" she asked.

Brew was grinning ear to ear. Roam was standing by her mom. He winked at her. She'd known he'd support whatever she wanted. He called her weekly or every other week just to check in.

Baron walked over and laid his hand on her shoulder. "You look so happy. If he is the man that puts that look on your face, then I guess I have another son."

Pit cleared his throat and then nodded. "Thanks, Baron. That means a lot to me. Sugar, do you want to hop down, and I can make it official for everyone to see?"

"Sugar! Why is she not hitting you for calling her that?" War asked.

"Because he says I'm sweet as sugar and strong as steel." Ariel unwrapped her legs from Pit and slid down to stand by him.

Pit motioned to Justice, and Justice whistled loudly to get everyone's attention. Not that she thought it was needed. She and Pit had been the spectacle everyone was watching.

"Ariel, you've given me hope. Will you be my Ol' Lady?" Pit asked.

"Yes."

Pit slipped the cut on her. The back had the Saint's Outlaws MC logo. The front of hers had Pit's Salvation. She turned back to him, and he was down on one knee.

"You know with you, I want it all. Ariel Shields, will you marry me tomorrow?"

She screamed yes and accepted the ring, though she wasn't sure anyone heard her answer. Once Pit had said tomorrow, Roam, War, and Baron had all screamed *what*?

Her mom didn't seem upset but then a couple times while they were shopping, her mom had a pensive look on her face at the outfits Ariel was trying on.

Pit slid his arm around her and turned toward the crowd. "Let's party tonight, but everyone's invited tomorrow to our wedding at two p.m., right here."

Pit's mom, Charlotte, came over to congratulate her. She pulled her in for a hug.

"Oh, I can tell you make him happy, which makes me happy. But I also know you obviously have no problem taking care of business when needed. You're exactly the type of daughter-in-law I wanted. Call me Charlie or Chuck."

Ariel couldn't be happier that Pit's mom welcomed her. "Thanks, Charlie. You've raised an amazing man."

His Aunt Ruth hugged her next. At some point, Ariel would probably need to share the history she knew all about so they'd feel safe talking to her, but for now, she was going to dance with her man.

As she and Pit danced, she noticed there were some women she assumed were Sirens, but it definitely wasn't the type of party she usually thought about for a one-percenter MC.

"Hey, do you think I'll need to make an example of one of the Sirens to make sure they understand you're off limits?"

Pit chuckled.

"Mom made the rule when they rebuilt that the Sirens had to leave a claimed man alone. If they tried anything, she'd boot them out. I haven't changed the rule because I don't need men in the MC who don't know what vows mean. If they'll cheat on their girlfriend or Ol' Lady, how can I know they'll keep our membership vows? I don't think you'll need to, but does it make me a pig that it sounds hot having you stake your claim?"

Ariel chuckled, leaning back and then rubbing against Pit's crotch.

"Seriously, Sugar? Are you trying to make me hard so your dad and brothers want to beat me?"

Ariel leaned up, kissing against Pit's neck. "Does it make me a pig that it sounds hot?"

Pit threw back his head, laughing. As the song ended, he led her over to the food.

"Let's eat!" he yelled.

CHAPTER FIVE

Although Ariel wanted to stay the night with Pit, she'd chosen to stay with her family. After the party, they'd all gathered in her mom's cabin that the girls were staying in for a family get-together. As long as it stayed cordial, Ariel would listen. If her block-headed older brothers were annoying, she might just bang some heads around.

She changed into the T-shirt and night shorts she had in her saddlebags. She detoured by the kitchen and grabbed a drink, then walked into the family room. She plopped down between Remi and her mom on the couch. Interestingly enough, all the men except Brew were sitting in a line. Were they planning an interrogation?

War started to speak, but her dad held his hand up.

"Ariel, I'm sorry if I ever made you feel you couldn't tell me about your life. I realize that I said one thing about women being able to do it all but when it came to my little girl, I didn't back up my words with my actions. Can you forgive me?"

Ariel jumped up and threw herself into her dad's arms.

"Always. I just wanted to be able to carve my own path. Remi and the bail bonds allowed me to do that."

Ariel sat back down and waited to see what was next.

"How did you two meet?" War asked.

Oh man. She could see this going south fast because it had been a little bit of a dust-up that night.

"I was checking out some different businesses with possible shady interests, and Pit, Justice, and Sledge were heading back to their compound from Pit's restaurant—a route they'd taken thousands of times. The business I was watching decided to attack Saint's for some reason. When I was watching the motorcycles come toward me, someone strung a chain across the road. When Pit and Justice passed my vehicle, they pulled the chain up. It yanked both Pit and Justice off their rides. Then someone started firing. I yelled and identified myself because I wanted them to hear and see me. I didn't want them to shoot, thinking I was a threat. Sledge told me to leave to stay safe. Instead, I drove my vehicle between the shooters and where Pit and Justice were on the ground. Sledge helped them get in, then followed me on his bike. Pit wanted to take me to dinner for helping them out, but I was leaving town. I said I'd collect another day."

War chuckled, then glanced toward Brew and laughed harder. Then Roam joined him.

"What are you all laughing about?" Ariel asked.

"We were hanging out in Texas, and I was mentioning I was worried about you. Brew told me to quit being such a worrier because you could take on anything that came your way. I nodded like I was agreeing, but secretly, I was calling bullshit. I guess in my mind, you're still the little sister I left when I went to the military. But he's obviously right—you've grown up. Pit was like the heroine in one of Remi's novels needing rescuing and you rescued him. What are they called, Remi?" War asked.

"A damsel in distress?" Remi questioned.

"Yeah, that's it, but you don't call a guy a damsel. What would you call it?"

"Let me check because this is hilarious and definitely fuel for teasing our future brother-in-law. Okay, it's saying the male version of damsel in distress is dude in distress. That doesn't seem right. Dude doesn't really fit Pit."

Ariel rolled her eyes. She wasn't sure if she was happy they weren't bugging her or irritated that they were trying to figure out some name to call Pit.

"Oh, I got it. So I put *Dude* into my online thesaurus and I came up with the perfect thing for Pit."

The glee on Brew's face made her want to punch him in the mouth. He was supposed to be her buddy, not Roam and War's. They were twins. They already had a built-in buddy.

"Okay, are you ready? Stud in distress. Get it? Because Mom and Dad will want grand-kids, and Pit will need to do his duty. Hey, maybe if Ariel still wants to work, then Pit could be a stay-at-home dad?"

"Brew, how some woman hasn't shot you yet is a miracle," Beth commented.

"Amen, sister," Sarah echoed.

There wasn't anything saying Pit might not want to be a stay-at-home dad, but Ariel wasn't having any of her brothers make Pit feel bad, especially not on their wedding day.

"If any of you neanderthals tell my hus-band-to-be or husband tomorrow about the dude in distress, stud in distress, or any variation thereof, I will get you back. You won't know when. You won't know how, and you definitely won't see it coming. Got it?"

Her brothers all nodded, but Brew had that look in his eyes that didn't bode well for her wedding day.

"Daddy, would you walk me down the aisle tomorrow?" Ariel asked.

"Do I have to dress up? You know I want to walk you, sweetie, but I only brought jeans."

"It's a biker wedding. Wear jeans and a nice, clean shirt." Ariel paused and stared at Brew."

"Oh, come on. One time I wore a shirt that smelled. Once. I'd spilled beer on my other stuff."

"I told Pit that I wanted us all together with him, my family, and good food," Ariel said.

Her mom smiled and so did her dad.

"Well, why don't you make a list of anything you need us to do for tomorrow? And then everyone should get some sleep. We've got a wedding to attend tomorrow," Regina said.

Ariel did what her mom asked, and it was great letting go of some of the items. She motioned Beth over when her brothers went back to their cabin.

"How much did they freak when the trackers started going every which way?"

Beth chuckled. "Let me show you. Sarah tapped into the camera where the guys were."

Beth started the video, and Ariel couldn't help but laugh. Watching her big, badass president brother run into the room carrying his little floofy dog, then rant and rave about his little sister being taken. Ariel felt a little guilty because trafficking wasn't anything to joke about, but she'd been so angry at them. She should have one of the girls mention some of the items she had on her wish list. Maybe they were feeling guilty enough she could milk them for a really nice present.

CHAPTER SIX

Ariel stood by her dad, waiting to start. Ariel told Pit all she needed was her man, but he wanted to get her something special. In the grassy area behind the clubhouse, he'd had a large white tent erected, half of it full of tables and chairs for eating and the other half having a dance floor. Crux and Cash, two of the officers of the club, were also handy with tools. They'd made a wooden arch, which had garlands of flowers on it. Pit stood under it in dark black jeans, his motorcycle boots, a white dress shirt, and his cut. The only thing missing that she usually saw on him was his sunglasses. She was excited she'd be able to look into his blue-grey eyes. She'd always heard the phrase *eyes are the window to the soul*. With Pit, she finally understood. Everything he was feeling for her was in his eyes.

She'd chuckled when she'd recognized who was officiating. Tack, the Sergeant at Arms for the club, was also on the SWAT team. One of his teammates' wives was a minister. Pit had come through, and Ariel was ready to marry her man.

Her dad held her arm and leaned down. "I want to share something with you. This today? This is the easy part. Pledging your love on a gorgeous day to the man you love. Other days will be hard. You might fight, or you might be dealing with money issues or health issues. Those are the days where you dig in and love. You love even when you're mad because true love, like what your mom and I have, doesn't come free. You've got to pay the price every day to keep your happily ever after."

Ariel leaned up to kiss her daddy's cheek. "Thank you. I've got good role models. I love Gavin, and I'll do whatever it takes to make it work."

Pit nodded at the DJ. *Highway to Hell* started playing.

"FNG, don't make me come beat you to play the right song!" Pit yelled.

"Stinger told me that was the song. I'm so sorry, Pres."

Stinger walked over and switched something, chuckling as he did. Ariel had kind of expected something. She'd grown up around an MC and joking was a part of club life. She would have walked down the aisle to *Highway to Hell* because she hadn't picked the music. She didn't care about that. She wanted to be Gavin's at night when they were in bed. During the day, she'd stand beside Pit, the MC President. The music started, and she smiled. He might be the tough MC President, but he was her soft, sweet man who adored her. And obviously knew every little thing about her if he knew the significance of this song.

"Dad, let's dance down the aisle."

Her dad smiled. As Bruno Mars' *Marry You* played, she and her dad danced down the aisle to her man. When they got to Pit, her dad kissed her cheek and then sat down with her mom. Pit took her hands in his and they turned toward the minister.

"Who gives this woman in marriage?" the minister asked.

"No one gives her to anyone. She's a fierce, badass woman who is choosing the man to spend her life with."

At her dad's words, the crowd screamed and yelled.

"I'm pretty fortunate you're choosing me because I don't think I'd survive without your love," Pit said.

"Well, I love you, and if you know me well enough that you pick a song from my favorite show without us talking about it, I think we're perfect for each other."

Pit listened to the minister's words and answered when appropriate, but if you asked him to describe the ceremony, the only thing he could say was how beautiful his bride was dancing toward him down the aisle.

He noticed every little thing about her. The way she squinted her eyes when he irritated her while she contemplated what she was going to do about it. The way she loved snuggling in bed and was so not a morning person. He'd only been able to notice it twice because she'd snuck away all the other times. And her heart was so big that she couldn't say no to anything. She donated to animal shelters, kids' athletic programs, and so many more. He could see her planning some poker runs or toy runs for them now that they were official.

What he couldn't wait for was knowing she wasn't leaving and he had her forever. He dreamed of taking her off on vacations but also of hosting everyone for holidays. And yeah, he imagined little ones with her eyes and his coordination. His woman was this badass, but put her in the bedroom, trying to walk to the bathroom, and she was the biggest klutz. She'd hit every dresser edge and sometimes the wall. How she snuck in places he'd never know, but she did.

To know that from today until forever, he got to show his amazing Sugar how much he loved her gave him peace. He looked forward to the coming years, getting to know her better, but he knew her pretty well. He'd learned what shows she liked, what music she danced to, and even her favorite foods. Since he'd planned the food, of course, they'd have barbecue from his restaurant, but he'd added some extra things she liked: onion rings from Red

Robin, along with Bloomin' Onions from Outback. He'd had burnt ends, chicken, ribs, brisket, and pulled pork brought in for the meat. His restaurant had a killer coleslaw and potato salad, which he and Ariel both loved.

Today was surreal because he'd wanted it to happen for forever and never dreamed it would come together so quickly.

"You may kiss the bride."

He slid his hands up to cup her face. "I love you, Sugar."

He kissed her and didn't care that everyone expected the short little wedding kiss. He hadn't kissed her all day. He poured everything he felt for her into the kiss—love, his devotion, and his happiness at her finally being his wife.

The yelling and clapping eventually had Ariel pulling back.

"Let's hold that thought. I'm really hungry. I was too nervous to eat much today," Ariel said.

After they'd eaten, the DJ had them dance their first dance. After that, his woman had danced with her dad, her brothers, and then his MC brothers had been dancing with her. Pit had danced with her mom, Regina, and his mom and aunt.

He glanced over at one of the tables and wondered if he needed to be worried. His mom and aunt were hanging out with all the Franks sisters. He'd heard all the stories of what they'd done over the years. He only hoped the city of Kansas City was still standing when they left.

The music changed to a pop song, and he checked to see where Ariel was. She was dancing toward him, then pulling him by his hand onto the dance floor. Then the little minx proceeded to rub against him as she basically used him like a stripper used a pole at a club. At least it wasn't a stripping number. The only thing that was probably saving him from her brothers not trying something was that she was dancing to *Can't Stop The Feeling*. He was pretty sure it was from a kids' movie. Then he decided maybe it was time to show her this old man could dance. He nodded at the DJ and then pulled her to him and spun her around.

Watching her move and dance with him, singing along to the song, had him grinning. She'd brought a lightness to his life when she'd steamrolled in with her love. He glanced around the dance floor. All the couples were dancing, which at least kept a fight from breaking out with her brothers. He swayed with her as the song slowed down, then dipped her back. Then he spun her away from him and then back.

"I love you, Gavin. Today was perfect!"

"I love you too. So much, Sugar."

CHAPTER SEVEN

Ariel laid there watching Gavin sleep as the sunlight came through the blinds. She had to admit that the old man had not only given her the wedding night of her dreams, but he'd tired her out. She felt just a tad guilty that when he'd tried to wake her at four this morning, she'd batted his hand away. She'd been a little sore between her legs because they'd made love twice before falling asleep. She still wasn't positive that Gavin just wasn't trying to prove a point that he could keep up with her at four because he'd acquiesced awfully quickly.

They were having a huge breakfast at the clubhouse. Gavin and she had decided, since they'd had such a quick wedding, that they weren't immediately leaving on a honeymoon. Besides, Thanksgiving was only a couple weeks away. She'd mentioned to her mom that she'd be having Thanksgiving at Saint's Outlaws MC but would definitely be home for Christmas. Liam, Roam's fiancée's brother, would be home on leave. They were planning a wedding on Christmas Day.

The other reason she was waiting on a honeymoon was that she and Pit were trying to get pregnant. She didn't want to plan and buy tickets only to be dealing with morning sickness. The restaurant catered, and since Pit had no idea they'd be getting married this weekend, his business had a huge amount of catering scheduled over the holiday season. They even had people special order smoked hams and smoked turkeys for the holiday season.

She snuck out of bed, leaving her husband asleep, and jumped in the shower. She wanted to see if she could get someone to help her move all her stuff to Pit's house today from her hotel room. Later, she could have them get the stuff from her small storage space.

She washed her hair and let the hot water help with her sore muscles. Pit had been a little energetic last night with his marking. She'd have to make sure her top covered where he'd given her multiple love bites.

She needed to get with Charlie and Ruth to see what had been planned for Thanksgiving. She knew some of the men would have to work the actual holiday. With Justice being the lawyer for the club and for other special cases, she guessed he wouldn't be working. Tack, the MC's Sergeant at Arms, was on the Kansas City SWAT team. She wasn't sure about his schedule. Stinger, the club's enforcer, ran their gun shop along with Crux, the Chaplain. She was guessing the gun range would be closed on Thanksgiving but open on Friday. She could see people going to the range and shopping for items.

Retread, who was the Road Captain, was a fire investigator. She was guessing that unless there was a huge fire, he'd be free. Sledge, the Secretary for the club, worked at a fire station. She'd check on his schedule too. Maybe the best thing to do would be to do a couple of meals scattered over Thursday, Friday, and Saturday to make sure everyone got to participate. As far as her investigations had gone, she didn't think most of the guys besides Pit and his cousins had family in town.

She also wanted to talk with Justice about his contacts with the hospitals and the battered women's shelter. That part of the Saint's business could expand even more with Ariel's contacts at the bail bonds. It would also be something she could do if and when she got pregnant because a lot of that job was research.

A slight sound and breeze heralded her husband coming into the shower with her. His arms slid around her, and he pulled her close.

"Love that I get to wake up to you every day, Sugar."

She breathed in Pit's musky scent and kissed his jaw. "Me too."

Pit grabbed Ariel's body wash she'd brought over and started washing her. When she looked at his face, he smiled.

"Not going to make love to you. I just want you to know how much you mean to me. We'll wait until you're not quite as sore."

His grin when he mentioned sore had her shaking her head.

"Proud of yourself, Old Man, that I had to say no during the night?"

Pit rinsed her, then took her mouth, kissing her until she didn't really care what his answer was.

"I'd never wish for you to be sore. I was just happy that I can keep up with my younger wife."

Ariel chuckled, then kissed Pit's lips. She squirted a little of his body wash in her hand

and proceeded to wash Pit as thoroughly as he washed her.

"Gavin, I do love you."

"Back at ya, Sugar!"

Pit listened to Ariel explain to her family that she'd be staying in Kansas City for Thanksgiving, but she'd be back for Christmas and Roam's wedding.

Pit was curious to experience Christmas Eve at Bluff Creek. Ariel had hinted there was something special about it. She also said she was going to invite any of the SOMC guys to attend if they'd like, along with his mom and aunt. Pit was already thinking through how to deal with the restaurant. It was doing phenomenally, so maybe they should have the pickups for the special stuff and then close for two to three days. He could even pay his employees extra so they weren't out any money.

Justice bumped him as he sat down beside Pit. "How's married life?"

"So far, so good, but then she hasn't had a chance to get irritated with me. I wouldn't change it for a thing," Pit replied.

"You're a brave man marrying one of the princesses of Bluff Creek," Retread said, joining them.

"I didn't marry the princess of Bluff Creek. I married the Queen of Saint's Outlaws," Pit said.

His brothers chuckled.

"Let's hope she doesn't decide you're too much trouble," Justice said.

"When did you become so grumpy about women?" Pit asked.

"I don't want to talk about it," Justice grumbled.

Pit got up and refilled his coffee, holding the pot up to see if War wanted more. War nodded, so Pit walked around the table. Pit had to admit that he wasn't the only one who looked like they were dragging today. He refilled War's, then Baron's when Baron held his cup up.

Pit marveled at the alliances Saint's had now, and it was all thanks to what his mom and aunt had done over the years. Of course, he'd fall in love with and marry a strong, fierce woman. He wanted the love his mom and dad had had, and he'd found it.

"If you guys are available, I thought you could help me move all my belongings from my hotel suite and my storage building," Ariel said.

War, Roam, and Brew stood up. "We are at your disposal, and we also want to buy you a really nice gift. Some of us to say they're sorry and me, just because I'm the best big brother. Figure out what you'd really like," Brew said.

"Oh, is there a price limit?" Ariel asked.

Pit grinned because he was positive Ariel was going to squeeze her brothers for a nicer gift.

"Brew is tossing in five hundred. He said that Roam and I need to pony up a thousand to show you that we're sorry," War muttered.

Pit joined in the laughter at War's expense.

"Well, let's get my stuff moved in. While we're working, I'll think about a proper congratulations and we're sorry present."

CHAPTER EIGHT

Ariel leaned back in her cozy enclosed back porch. She chuckled when she thought about her brothers' faces when she'd told them about the wedding present they were gifting her. With Brew's construction experience and their twenty-five hundred dollars, she'd checked with Gavin about having the guys enclose the covered part of their deck with windows that could be all screen or switched out with solid glass for the winter months.

Besides being a great present for them, it had cemented a great working relationship with the Saint's and the Bluff Creek men.

Pit had asked for volunteers to help, and it had turned into a project all of them worked on.

Her parents, Charlie, and Ruth had decided that, in addition to the presents they'd already bought the couple, they would fill the room with furniture. Ariel had gone with them to a furniture store and picked out the items. Brew had also made a surprise for Ariel in one area. He'd crafted a huge hanging bed so Ariel could lie out there and read. Brew had rolled his eyes when some of the Saint's brothers had teased Pit about having fun with Ariel on it. Oh yeah, she planned on taking advantage of her husband out there. But it was also a great place for them to hang out in the winter when Pit wanted to smoke or grill something.

Even though he could get his stuff from the restaurant, he still enjoyed smoking briskets or pork butts at home.

Ariel was looking forward to baking with the huge kitchen she now had. She and Pit had seen her family off, and Pit had left to check on his restaurant. Her family had stayed the rest of the week to help with the build. Today was Friday, and she was looking forward to her first weekend alone with her husband. She looked through the trees toward the back of Pit's property and saw Charlie and Ruth making their way across the backyard. She stood up and opened the door to the porch to let them in.

Charlie glanced toward the main part of the house.

"Pit left to check the restaurant," Ariel said.

Charlie nodded and sat down in one of the chairs. Ruth sat down on the loveseat across from Ariel.

"Now that you're family, we wanted to share something with you," Charlie mentioned, then stared at Ruth. Ruth didn't say anything right away. Ariel hated seeing her so uncomfortable.

"That Ruth is Ruthless, the SOMC bogeyman of Kansas City?" Ariel asked.

Charlie and Ruth stared at her. "How'd you know?"

"When I became interested in Pit, I investigated the club. I know they are one-percenters, but I wanted to make sure it was a type of one-percenters I could live with. In researching the time the guys were away in the military, I noticed when Ruthless was spotted and when Ruthless wasn't. I'm amazed at how you both held the club together when you had to be grieving."

Charlie leaned over and patted Ariel's hand. "Thank you. We did it because we didn't have a choice. We weren't going to let those boys lose out on their legacy."

"Yes, and we also weren't going to let someone who trafficked women claim the territory," Ruth said. "Though I have to admit, playing Ruthless let me get some of the anger out about how our men were betrayed."

Ariel could understand the grief and the anger. She'd only been married for less than a week. If someone took Pit from her, she'd burn the world to get justice. She couldn't imagine how scared Charlie and Ruth had been and how worried they were about what was next.

"I was actually going to come chat with you about it anyway. I know Pit and the guys haven't figured out why they were targeted. I think it might be time for Ruthless to take credit again for a couple of things to put some fear in people. We might not know who they were, but we know what building they were using. I'm positive the shell corporation that owns it isn't above board. I've been thinking."

The grins on Charlie and Ruth's faces told Ariel they were more than on board with her idea. She smiled, then laid out her plan.

Kansas City would be as safe as she could make it for any of their future children. Hopefully, Pit would understand what she had to do. He had to know when he married her the type of person she was.

CHAPTER NINE

Pit stared around the table. Ariel had organized three different Thanksgiving meals along with a couple of deliveries to those in need and first responders who were working the holiday. Tonight, the Saturday after Thanksgiving, had been when all the MC brothers were off work.

The smoked ham and smoked turkey were from his restaurant. His mom had made her sweet potatoes and dressing. Ariel had taken charge of the desserts because she loved baking. His aunt had made her cheesy potato casserole along with mashed potatoes and gravy. When she mentioned just making her cheesy potatoes, FNG, their prospect, had mentioned he'd never had homemade mashed potatoes and gravy. Ruth couldn't stand that he hadn't experienced it, so she'd made both.

Pit had so many reasons to be thankful. He'd fallen in love and married a fierce, loving woman. His brothers were gathered around the table, and they hadn't lost anyone this year. His mom and aunt were walking around with smiles on their faces at the possibility of grandkids at some point. His Sugar wasn't pregnant yet, but it wasn't for lack of trying on their part. Hopefully, it would happen soon, but if not, he was willing to have kids with his Sugar however she wanted. There were plenty of kids in the world who needed a home.

Pit stood up and waited for the group to quiet down. "You know I'm not big on sharing feelings."

He paused because his brothers jeered and yelled so loudly.

"But my Sugar has changed some of that. I wanted to share how thankful I am to be brothers with all of you. We've weathered some storms but come through on the other side. We've helped people find new lives where they are safe. As we head into the holiday season, which brings its own ups and downs for those of you who are first responders, I want to say thank you. I couldn't ask for a better brotherhood than my brothers here."

Pit raised his glass and toasted their brotherhood, their family. Then he sat down, and they started passing the food.

He watched his mom, aunt, and wife. Yesterday evening, while he was helping at the restaurant, the building where they'd been ambushed burned to the ground. Surprisingly, none of the buildings beside it caught on fire because they'd been miraculously wet down ahead of time. Witnesses all mentioned a masked, ninja-like figure seen in the area before the fire started. But it was the large, black capital R spray-painted on the ground in front of the building that had him wondering what his wife and family were doing while he was at work.

He should have known when he married the Bluff Creek badass princess that she'd make sure people knew not to mess with the Saint's Outlaws MC. Now he just needed to work on her sharing stuff like that with him ahead of time. He knew she was capable of protecting herself, but he wanted to be a part of protecting her. She didn't have to do everything on her own anymore. Maybe he'd just ramp her up a couple times and hold off letting her finish until she agreed to at least let him know what was happening.

He smirked at his wife. Yep, that's what he'd do. And boy, would it be fun convincing her.

Ariel held onto the headboard and debated if she'd go to jail if she killed her husband. She was positive if she had women on the jury, they'd understand. If he pulled his mouth away one more time before she was ready to come, she might just beat him.

"Now, Sugar, you know all you have to do is agree, and I'll make you come so hard you'll see stars," Gavin breathed against her.

He was millimeters away from where she wanted—no, craved—his mouth, or his cock, or any other freaking appendage that would help her come.

Ariel decided she was done playing his game and let go of the headboard. Although she adored her husband and his dominant ways most times, she wouldn't set a precedent where he used sex to coerce her to agree to anything. He needed to talk with her, and they could work together.

"Sugar, do I need to tie your hands there?"

Ariel slid her hands to Gavin's face and stared into his eyes.

"I love you so much, Gavin," she said, then slid her hands down to his chest, pushing him over and jumping up. She wasn't going to make this easy. If she wasn't going to get to come, so be it. She wasn't agreeing to anything under duress. She stood by the side of the bed and grabbed her robe, sliding it on and cinching the tie.

"Since you seem to not be in the mood to finish, I'm assuming you're having a little performance issue. Let's table this for another evening," Ariel said, walking into the bathroom and closing the door.

She listened to see if she could hear her husband. She was positive he couldn't ignore the challenge she'd laid down. That would teach him to try to coerce her agreement by withholding orgasms. She walked over to the mirror, smoothed her hair, made sure her face didn't look as if she was planning something, and then opened the bathroom door. Pit was standing by the bed, blocking the door out of the room.

"Really, Gavin, it's okay. Let's just go heat up dinner."

He stalked toward her with his eyes full of determination. She hoped he understood she wasn't getting back in that bed without a guarantee he wasn't going to be an ass.

He slid his hand into her hair, tugging her head to the side, then trailing his lips up her neck to her ear.

"Sugar, if you promise me that you'll tell me about anything that might go sideways, then I'll promise never to try to coerce your agreement when we're in bed. I know you're a freaking badass, but the man in me needs to know I'm keeping you safe too."

Well, fudge. Of course, he'd want something in exchange. Her mom had told her marriage was about give and take. It looked like it was time for her to give a little.

"I promise," Ariel whispered against Gavin's ear and slid her arms around him.

"That's all I ask," Gavin said, lifting her over his shoulder and smacking her butt. "Now let's see about those orgasms."

Ariel got a little dizzy as Gavin flipped her over on the bed and removed her robe. She leaned up to catch his lips. Gavin kissed her back and deepened the kiss. Settling himself between her thighs, she slid her hands across his chest, then around his back.

She didn't want slow. She didn't want sweet. She wanted her husband inside her now. He'd become the man she couldn't live without, and she loved when he was soft and sweet. She also freakin' loved when he was a little rougher, as if he couldn't control himself. Sure, she'd make sure that she told him if she was going into danger, as long as he did too. She'd wait to drop that little bit until after Gavin fulfilled his husbandly duty.

Gavin notched himself at her entrance, then cocked his head to the side. "What's that little grin?" he asked.

"It's my *I want my husband's cock* look mixed with *I'm going to kill him if he doesn't get inside me*," she replied.

Gavin smirked, then slowly, ever so slowly, pushed inside, then gave her more of his weight, pinning her beneath him. She trembled, her hard nipples brushing against Gavin's chest hair. Everything about this man did it for her. She hoped when they were blessed with kids, that they were boys with Gavin's eyes and smile.

"Sugar, you seem a little distracted," Gavin growled and then proceeded to make sure she was focused only on him.

This is what she wanted. What she craved. The intimacy and connection with him. His thrusts sped up, and she was moving with him, shivers racing through her as he built her higher, racing toward completion.

"I fuckin' love you, Sugar," Gavin growled as he came. She couldn't say anything besides groaning his name as everything coalesced inside her and detonated.

CHAPTER TEN

Pit followed Ariel into the snowplow
barn. Christmas Eve in Bluff Creek
was beautiful. It was a clear night with no
clouds. The night sky was filled with twin-
kling stars. It was cold but not freezing.
Tonight was some secret that the MC was
allowing him, Ariel, his mom, aunt, and
Justice to be a part of. They were spend-
ing Christmas Eve and Christmas at Bluff
Creek because Ariel's brother Roam was
getting married tomorrow.

Ariel had been in a strange mood, and he
wondered if his woman was hiding something. The month since Thanksgiving had

been busy with the restaurant. Ariel had traveled a couple times when Rose had needed backup on a job. He hadn't met Rose until they'd arrived today. Rose was a former police officer who was also one of Scoop's younger sisters. She and her sister Tasha were twins, and talk about twins being so different. Rose was rougher and harder, whereas Tasha was in nursing and softer.

If his Sugar was going to be backing up someone, he'd want it to be Rose. She seemed to be able to handle herself well.

He glanced around the barn that tomorrow would be where Roam and Sprite said *I do*. It seemed like an extremely busy weekend: the secret thing tonight, present opening at lunch at the clubhouse, and then a wedding in the evening.

In an effort to hopefully garner some space from his father-in-law, Pit had brought a huge amount of smoked meats for the Christmas Day meal and the wedding. Baron seemed to have this habit of just dropping in and checking on Ariel as if he thought Pit was going to kill her and hide her body somewhere.

He adored his woman. Although her father was driving him up the wall, he wouldn't retaliate against Baron yet. Of course, if the visits continued, Pit might change his mind.

Everyone had gathered in a circle. War whistled to get everyone's attention.

"Last year, I remember showing up to this meeting wondering why the heck, as Bluff Creek Brotherhood MCs President, I didn't know what was happening. For those of you who are new, I'd like to welcome you to the Santa's Slay MC. This secret MC is only active on Christmas Eve. It was formed thirteen years ago when my mom, Regina, and her best friend, Kathryn, who was dying, decided that Christmas Eve would be a time of changing lives and bringing hope to those who need it. Tonight you'll be Santa's helpers, making sure that you help others."

Pit listened to War explain more about how Santa's Slay MC functioned and all the rules for tonight. He had to admit he got a little teary-eyed listening to all of them take the vow to embody love to those you meet. Ariel leaned over and wrapped an arm around his waist. He slid his arm around her shoulders and hugged her.

He wondered if this was something they could do Christmas Eve in Kansas City if they weren't able to make it home. Everyone needed hope. He glanced over at Justice, his mom, and aunt. His mom nodded, and he knew she was thinking the exact same thing.

He shrugged on the Santa's Slay MC cut they provided and then stared at his beautiful Sugar as she situated the Santa hat on his head. He and Ariel picked up the red Santa bags filled with presents. When they got out to the bikes, he saw that some of them had been modified with racks. His already had a special carrier. When he'd replaced his bike that had been wrecked when Ariel rescued him, he'd had a special rack built so he could carry the pans his restaurant used if needed. When he wasn't using them, they looked like any rack on a motorcycle. When he needed the larger rack, he just flicked a little lock and the longer pieces slid out to be used.

He watched Ariel secure the sack since she'd done that before, then got on the bike with her behind him. He followed her instructions to the first house. The smiles on the faces and the gratitude in everyone's eyes made him feel ten feet tall. Although they were giving to people, Pit was receiving so much in return.

It took him and Ariel about two hours to finish their bags. Bluff Creek was organized and had trucks with more bags at loading points along the road. If Ariel decided she wanted to do something like this in Kansas City, they might need to start planning soon.

He parked his motorcycle in front of the house they were staying at. He and Ariel were staying with her parents along with his mom and aunt. He wanted to end the night with him inside Ariel, but Baron had put them in the room right next to them. He wasn't sure if his father-in-law would try to kill him if he made the princess of the MC scream out Pit's name as she came.

Ariel got off the motorcycle and then held her hand out to him. He took her hand and then followed as his Sugar led him around the house and out toward some trees behind her parents' house. The cold, crisp air and silence surrounded them. He could hear motorcycles as people returned home, but otherwise, the night was quiet. Ariel paused close to the trees but in the middle of the field. He glanced around to see if he could figure out what she was doing.

Ariel turned until they were facing each other. It was dark out, and he could barely see his Sugar's face. She pulled out a little wrapped package and her phone.

"Open this," she said, putting it in his hand and then turning the light on so he could see what he was opening. He ripped the paper and then stared at the stick inside of a plastic bag. He flipped it over and stared at the word – *Pregnant*. When he looked up at her, she smiled, "Merry Christmas, Gavin."

He grasped her by the back of her neck, pulling her close and kissing her lips. He was equal parts scared and excited. He poured it all into his kiss, trying to let her know how much she and their baby meant to him. His Sugar, his salvation, had brought the MC President the best Christmas present ever.

When he pulled back, he couldn't keep from asking, "How far along?"

She smiled at him, touching his cheek. "It's early yet. I'm barely two weeks overdue for my period. Can we keep it just between us until we're further along?"

He pulled her close, holding her tight as if he could keep her safe and well.

"We can do whatever you want because my Sugar is giving me the dream."

CHAPTER ELEVEN

Pit waited as his wife finished putting on her makeup. Why, when she swiped the lipstick on her lower lip, did it make him want to muss her all up again? He knew that wasn't a possibility. Her brother was getting married today. Pit and Ariel were in charge of the kids making it down the aisle as the ring bearers and flower girls. He only hoped he and Ariel could keep them all wrangled.

Ariel's news last night had him looking at the kids differently. Roam and Sprite's minions had scared him, but holding little Matthew had him imagining a little boy or a little girl with his and Ariel's features. He stood and waited until she was done, then held his arm out.

"Shall we go wrangle the kids? It will be good experience," he said quietly. Their door was closed, but he wasn't chancing anyone finding out when Ariel wanted it quiet.

"Yes, let's head over there. Mom said we could take Roam and Sprite's side-by-side because it has the car seats already installed."

He followed his woman downstairs, then to the living room where the kids were all waiting. It took a little bit to get them all in car seats or seatbelts, along with all the little wedding things they needed: flower girl baskets, ring bearer pillows, and shoes. Oakley and Georgia kept kicking off their shoes. He finally slid them into a little bag he ran back into the house to get. If they kept kicking them off and he had to stop on the drive, they'd never make it in time.

Once they had all the kids ready to go, he had a huge amount of respect for Roam and Sprite to wrangle this many children day after day. Blake, their six-year-old, had definitely helped. She was a junior bridesmaid and was going to carry Matthew down the aisle until she got to Regina. Then Regina would hold him during the ceremony. Grant, who was four and a half—because the half was apparently very important—was carrying the rings along with his younger brother Casper. Pit was thankful the rings were tied on the pillow because he'd stopped Grant from hitting his sisters with it or from him and Casper playing football with the pillow. Georgia, Casper's twin, and Oakley, who was close to the same age, were flower girls.

It was Pit's job to make sure the kids got down the aisle because Sugar was Sprite's matron of honor since she was the only female sibling. War was Roam's best man, and Brew was officiating. Ariel had mentioned Brew had decided to get the certification to be able to perform weddings in Texas and Kansas.

His Sugar was smiling at him, and he winked back. Liam, Sprite's brother who was home on leave for the wedding and Christmas, helped Sprite off the trike he'd ridden over to bring her. Pit had to stare a minute at Sprite's dress before he realized it wasn't white. It was a pale pink to match her hair. To him, she looked exactly like a princess. The smile on her face was so wide.

"Sprite, are you ready for me to tell them to start the music?" Pit asked.

"Yes," Sprite said.

He turned and nodded. The music started. It took him a minute to recognize it. He and Ariel had attended the Trans-Siberian Orchestra's Christmas concert a couple weeks ago. His Sugar had loved this song and hummed along to it, so he'd made sure he knew what it was—Christmas Canon. This was an instrumental version, and he wished he could dance with Ariel in his arms instead of wrangling children.

He motioned for Blake and Matthew to go. Roam needed to make sure he had plenty of firepower when she got older. He'd be chasing the boys away. Once she'd handed Matthew to Regina, he sent Grant and Casper with the ring bearer pillows. When they were halfway down the aisle, he could see that this wasn't going to go great. Grant accidentally bumped Casper, at least he hoped it was an accident, and them going down the aisle nicely was over. Casper grunted, scowled, and then pushed Grant. Bear, who was sitting in an aisle seat, caught the boys and separated them. Whatever he said must have worked because they straightened up and walked down the aisle.

After seeing the boys, Sprite asked Ariel to walk with the girls down the aisle to avoid any mishaps. He kissed her cheek as she and the girls headed down the aisle. Then he got ready to open the doors wider for Sprite and her brother, Liam. The music changed just a little as Liam walked Sprite down the aisle. Pit waited until they were through the doors, then shut them after them. He walked around and sat down in the seat they'd saved for him in the family row.

He sat there, not really listening much, until the couple said their vows.

"I, Sprite Jane Pacer, take you, Roam Matthew Shields, to be my husband. To have and to hold with love, laughter, and sometimes tears. To remember that no matter where I am or what I'm going through, you and I are stronger together."

Pit could see why Roam had tears in his eyes because Sprite's words touched Pit.

"I, Roam Matthew Shields, take you, my lovely Sprite Jane Pacer, to be my wife. From this day forward until I cease to breathe on this earth. You have brought love and laughter into my life and made what was a house our home. I will dry your tears and work every day to remind you how incredible you are and that we are stronger together. These words I so vow."

Although Sprite was still smiling, tears were trickling down her cheeks. Roam leaned close and kissed her face, then pulled out a handkerchief and wiped her tears.

"With these vows, I now pronounce you husband and wife. You may seal your union with a kiss," Brew said.

Pit stared past Roam and Sprite to his wife. He mouthed *I love you, Sugar* to her. He sniffed because he was not going to cry. But seeing her so happy and knowing she cradled their little one inside her had him wanting to hold her in his arms.

She mouthed back *I love you too* and his world was perfect. His MC might be on the other side of the law, but he would do whatever it took to keep her and their child safe. Their business of not-so-legal gun sales allowed them to be close to the underbelly without being completely a part of it. It was an excellent cover for their helping women escape abuse.

His MC worked closely with the Franks sisters' organization to help individuals escape abusive situations. Neither organization followed the law when helping people get away, but sometimes things had to be done for the greater good.

When they'd lost his dad, he'd hoped that when he was President of the Saint's Outlaws MC, he would have a safer MC. He wanted to lead them to a future where their sons or daughters could prosper.

He stood up as Ariel walked over to him. He slid his arm around her.

"Your mom didn't say. Are we supposed to pick up anything here before heading to the reception?"

Ariel just smiled and leaned up close to his ear, "How about I show you all the places we can hide and maybe kiss before the reception?"

Pit nodded. Hide and kiss sounded good because after wrangling kids, his Sugar deserved a little surprise. He followed her out the door because he would follow Ariel to the ends of the earth; she made his life complete.

EPILOGUE- AUGUST 10TH, 2025

Ariel sat by Pit, opening the last baby gift. Thank goodness she only had about three weeks left before her due date because this summer had been miserable. Now, all the guys had been amazing, but the heat, the sweating, and her huge belly had made her feel like a friggin' beached whale. Plus, she had hemorrhoids to deal with because she'd been in the car, sitting too much on trips to Bluff Creek. No one warned her about that, which was a load of crap. But there had been some huge things happening that she couldn't miss, and she wouldn't have missed for anything.

Pit had worried about the swelling in her feet, so he'd put a little stool for her legs to be up on while they opened presents. He was going to be the best dad. He already had a lot of practice with being an uncle. She could still remember Justice's face that day when his life changed.

She'd already seen Justice's soft side even though he rocked his harsh lawyer face most times. His little one had him tied in knots but in the best way. Pit was thrilled that Justice's son and their son would grow up together.

Pit's face at the ultrasound had been delighted, but she still teased him sometimes about his comment about his son being so well-endowed and taking after his father. Men. Ariel was relieved she wasn't having a little girl, though she wouldn't mind one later. Ariel had hoped for a boy because growing up, she had been safe because of her older brothers, and she couldn't think of anything better than that for her own kids.

Her little boy would have plenty of leather. Between all the brothers and both families, their little one had three pairs of toddler motorcycle boots, infant and toddler leather jackets, and so many onesies with sayings about bikers. She loved their family.

Pit hadn't had any more trouble lately. At least she didn't think so. He hadn't mentioned it, and he'd promised to try to warn her if they did. He'd become even more protective of her when she started showing.

She'd backed off of work and everything she did now was online for Franks and

Daughters Bail Bonds. She and Pit had talked with her family about Santa's Slay MC. Everyone had thought it was a fantastic idea to have chapters in different cities to help people. Once Cider Creek had heard what the SOMC was doing, Bootstrap had said he wanted to do the same in Texas. Christmas 2025 would have three chapters of Santa's Slay MC bringing hope and joy to people on Christmas Eve.

Ruth and Charlie walked over. "Ariel, how about a little break between gifts? You could have a drink and maybe a snack."

Ariel nodded. "Thanks and a bathroom break would be great."

At her words, Pit was there, grasping her hand and helping her up. She kissed him on the cheek and waddled to the bathroom. And she was definitely waddling, though she didn't want anyone to tell her how cute it was. She might have been in a little bit of a bad mood when Cue asked her why she was walking funny the other day. After she'd thrown a bowl toward his head, he'd apologized and then delivered piping hot barbecue for supper that evening and the next.

She was surprised Pit hadn't followed her into the bathroom. When he had to help her out of bed at night, he followed her in and then helped her up afterward. Her mom had warned her that when you had a baby, all modesty was lost at delivery. Heck, she'd lost all modesty now. Pit had shaved her legs for her the other day because there was no way she could reach her lower legs.

Of course, her man had made it into sexy time, which was fine by her. Her third trimester of pregnancy had made her hornier than before. Pit was always up for satisfying her cravings for him. They only had two positions that were comfortable for her, though—on her side lying down with Pit behind her or on her hands and knees. She was looking forward to when her man could toss her down on the bed and crawl on top of her. Who knew she'd be craving missionary style? She'd tried to ride him a month ago and lifting up her huge belly had made it more work than fun.

She finished up and washed her hands, then dried them. It sounded like the party was getting louder. She walked out, and Tack was standing at the door asking for Justice, but he was in his uniform.

"Does somebody need Justice to represent them?" Ariel asked.

Tack shook his head. "No, the police are outside. They need Justice. He's wanted for questioning."

"Questioning for what?" Ariel asked, though she didn't think anyone heard her over all the commotion.

Justice walked out of the kitchen and handed some items to Pit, then leaned over close and whispered something in his ear. Pit nodded. Justice walked out the front door. Ariel tried to see, but Crux had placed himself in front of her.

"We need you and the baby safe. Even though they said they are doing it peacefully, all it takes is one hothead deciding he feels threatened," Crux said. "Tack heard what was happening and came along because he promised he could keep it calm."

Ruth and Charlie came up beside her. "You should call Scoop and Sarah, Ariel, and see if they can get us any info."

Ariel nodded. She was worried about Justice. She wasn't sure what was going on, but she was positive her man would have it under control as soon as possible. She could trust Pit because he'd given her the world.

She'd hoped the last couple weeks before she had the baby would be calm but obviously that wasn't to be. What the heck had happened that they were taking Justice in?

I hope you loved Pit and Ariel's story. Justice is available for preorder and if you've not dived into the Bluff Creek Brotherhood MC, what are you waiting for? You can find all about my books, FB group- Nat Logan's Bluff Creek Beauties, FB page and what's going on right here:

Printed in Great Britain
by Amazon

57657342R00086